JF-G7

DATE DUE

DATE DUE

DEC 22 2003	JAN 1 6 2004
JUL 1 6 2004	MAR 3 0 2004
DEC 2 6 2004	

DEMCO, INC. 38-2931

Redbir d

at Rockefeller Center

by Peter Maloney and Felicia Zekauskas

Dial Books for Young Readers New York

To
26 The Fairway
Cedar Grove, New Jersey
Sideyard

Published by Dial Books for Young Readers
A Division of Penguin Books USA Inc.
375 Hudson Street
New York · New York 10014

Designed by Pamela Darcy and Zinc
Printed in Hong Kong
First Edition
1 3 5 7 9 10 8 6 4 2

Library of Congress Cataloging in Publication Data
Maloney, Peter.
Redbird at Rockefeller Center/by Peter Maloney and Felicia Zekauskas.
p. cm.
Summary: Kate is heartbroken when her favorite tree is cut down
and shipped off to Rockefeller Center for its Christmas use, along with
the bird who has been living in the tree.
ISBN 0-8037-2256-7 (trade).—ISBN 0-8037-2257-5 (library)
[1. Trees—Fiction.   2. Birds—Fiction.   3. Environmental protection—Fiction.
4. Christmas—Fiction.   5. Stories in rhyme.]   I. Zekauskas, Felicia.   II. Title.
PZ8.3.R24445Ne   1997   [E]—dc21   96-45728   CIP   AC

The illustrations were created with pencil, watercolor, and gouache.

There once was a tree of a height to astound
That people could see for miles around.

It towered above the house of a lady
Who found it too tall and overly shady.

"It's crowding our yard!" she cried out loud.

"There's only one way it could make us all proud.

Rockefeller Center could use a big spruce—

Our tree would be perfect for their Christmas use!"

Kate tried her best to change her mom's mind:
"To chop down this tree would be very unkind!
There's chirping and tweeting and whistling within.
I'm sure there are birds living out on a limb!"

"About such creatures I don't give a pittance.
That tree is going and I say good riddance!
What do I care for a dumb bird or two—
I'd much rather have a beautiful view!"

The next day a man in a truck pulled in front
And eyeing the tree he let out a grunt.
He drew back his ax and gave it a whack,
And up at the tip a little egg cracked.

When the tree hit the ground, it rattled the street,
And after it crashed, Kate heard a small tweet.
She spotted a nest and the tiniest red thing.
"My goodness," she cried, "I think it's a fledgling!"

But the driver worked fast and the next thing Kate knew
The tree, truck, and Redbird had vanished from view.
They sped through the snow, then under a river . . .

The driver had something he had to deliver:
That thousand-foot spruce, that giant green tree
Was scheduled to be in the city by three!

The tree was put up before you could wink,
Next to that world-famous ice-skating rink.
It reached toward the heavens, then started to taper;
Its tip was as high as the tallest skyscraper!

The Ladies Auxiliary all worked together
And decked out the tree with birds of a feather.
Someone had gotten it into her head
To fill up the tree with birds that were red!

The tree was a beauty, the best one in years,
And all would agree it was worthy of cheers.
But while skaters went 'round, gliding and falling,
No one could hear a small Redbird calling.

"I say, c'mon, please, someone open your beak!
A thousand redbirds and not one who will speak?
Can't anyone help me, I'm so far from home,
Why must you all make me feel so alone?"

But no bird responded—they weren't just bluffing.
How could they speak? They were nothing but stuffing!

The days left till Christmas flew by without stopping
In a flurry of snowflakes and holiday shopping.
The season was joyous, the whole world seemed glad—
Except for two hearts that were sadder than sad.

"Let go of that tree, Kate!
It's gone and that's that!
There's nothing to do, dear,
It's not coming back!
Why must you have
These Christmastime blues—
Good heavens, our tree
Was just shown on the news!"

"Mother, believe me,
There's life in that tree—
I tell you I'm certain
I heard a bird plea!"

"I've got it, I'll prove it, I know what we'll do—
We'll visit that tree up on Fifth Avenue.
I'll show you those birds are not living at all—
They're no more alive than a Christmas tree ball."

So they went and they waited and heard not a peep.
Wouldn't you know it, Redbird was asleep.

"I'm sorry, my darling, it's time you faced facts.
Now let's do some shopping at Bergdorf's and Saks!
We'll get a few things and then we should leave.
It's getting much later and it *is* Christmas Eve."

They shopped for an hour, then as they departed,
Katie cried out, "I'm so brokenhearted!"

Now who can explain how snowflakes and tears
Falling together can awaken deaf ears?
Sometimes two things together can do
Something that makes the impossible true.

Each snowflake and tear awakened a bird
And slowly but surely a thousand wings stirred.
The tree was a-twitter, a chorus of peeping,
They'd all come alive as if wakened from sleeping!

They wanted to help and one had a plan—
He said to Redbird, "We'll all lend a hand.
Tonight's Christmas Eve, we've got you a gift,
We'll help you go home, we'll give you a lift!"

Then all of the birds gripped the limbs where they perched,
And beating their wings, the mighty tree lurched.
It rose from its stand like a giant green rocket.
(Thank goodness that no one had bothered to lock it!)

The tree weighed a ton, but flapping together
The birds all agreed it was light as a feather.
"Now that we're airborne and high in the sky,
Please tell us, Redbird: Just where should we fly?"

"I'm hearing a voice inside of my head.
I think it's a prayer being said in a bed.
And though I can't give a street name or address,
Let's follow that voice, let's keep flying west!"

So while mothers and fathers and children all snored,
One thousand redbirds flew westward and soared.
The tree crossed the sky, then made a soft landing
In the very same spot where it used to be standing.

When Katie awoke at a quarter past dawn,
There was more than fresh snow out there on the lawn.
Where once there had been a sad vacancy,
Now again stood Kate's favorite old tree.

"Mother, come quickly, get out of your bed!
We've got a few guests who will have to be fed."
Her mother blinked twice, then swallowed real hard.
She said, "That darn tree must belong in our yard."

"And I'm happy to say we've got just what we need:
A thousand-pound sack of Redbird birdseed!
It wasn't a gift I expected at all—
But that Santa Claus, he's right on the ball!"

Their Christmas was joyous and Kate summed it up
While sipping eggnog from her favorite cup:
"A White Christmas is lovely, but this year instead

I'm so very happy our Christmas turned red."